The Case of the
Frog-jumping Contest

Read all the Jigsaw Jones Mysteries

And Don't Miss . . .

The Case of the
Frog-jumping Contest

by James Preller
illustrated by Jamie Smith
cover illustration by R. W. Alley

A
LITTLE APPLE
PAPERBACK

SCHOLASTIC INC.
New York Toronto London Auckland Sydney
Mexico City New Delhi Hong Kong Buenos Aires

ISBN 0-439-67805-6

12 11 10 9 8 7 6 5 4   5 6 7 8 9 10/0

Printed in the U.S.A.   40
First printing, May 2005

For Lisa, just because.
—JP

CONTENTS

The Case of the
Frog-jumping Contest

Chapter One

Stringbean

"My frog is missing," croaked Stringbean Noonan. "And I MUST have him back by this Sunday at noon."

"Sunday at noon?!" Mila exclaimed. "That's only twenty-four hours from now."

Stringbean stuffed two dollars into my coin jar. "There's more where that came from," he sniffed. "Just find that frog."

I glanced at my partner, Mila Yeh, who was sitting beside me. Together, we were as high as an elephant's eye. That is: We were in my tree house, swaying in the spring

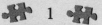

breeze. I think the wind made Stringbean a little nervous. His real name was Jasper, but most kids called him Stringbean because he's so skinny. I wondered if Stringbean was afraid he'd blow away.

"This frog," I finally said, "I'm guessing he was, um, some sort of pet."

Stringbean frowned. "Adonis, my frog, is much more than a pet," he told us. "He's a champion."

"A champion frog," I murmured.

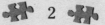

I scribbled a quick picture of a frog in my detective journal. Too bad it looked like an upside-down sock with eyeballs. Yeesh.

It's hard to draw something when you aren't sure what that something looks like. I mean, really sure. The fact is I hadn't taken a real good look at a frog lately. Or, like, *ever*. Who stares at frogs, anyway? I don't spend my afternoons hanging around lily pads.

Beneath the drawing I wrote:

Find Kermit.
Sunday, noon.
RIBBIT.

I poured myself a tall glass of grape juice. I don't know why, but the detective business often brings out the loonies. I've solved mysteries about mummies, glow-in-the-dark ghosts, and buried treasure. I figured that a frog wouldn't be so tough. I offered juice to Mila and Stringbean. They weren't thirsty.

Mila spoke up. "What's so important about noon on Sunday?" she asked Stringbean. "Why do you need Adonis by then?"

Stringbean reached into his back pocket. Then he handed a piece of blue paper to Mila:

FROG-JUMPING CONTEST

✷ ✷ ✷

To be held Sunday, April 25, at 12:00

BRING YOUR OWN FROG!

AGES 3-5 Can have some help in circle
AGES 6-9 Cannot be aided in any way
AGES 10 and up Cannot be aided in any way

Trophies for 1st and 2nd place
Ribbons for all participants
$20 Cash Prize for longest jump

"Twenty dollars," I whistled. "That's a lot of money."

"Adonis is a lot of frog," Stringbean replied. "He could win that contest, easy."

Stringbean told us all about it. Every year he went to this big county fair. There were rides and animals and all sorts of

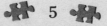

stuff. Anyway, that's how he got into this whole frog-jumping way of life.

"Twenty-four hours isn't a lot of time," I said to Stringbean. I turned to Mila. "We'll need to do the usual missing-pet routine. Make posters. Look around the neighborhood. Talk to witnesses."

Mila nodded. She smiled hopefully at Stringbean. "We handle missing-pet cases all the time," she said.

"Of course," I added, "it's usually a

missing dog or cat. This will be our first frog." I smiled. "But don't worry, I'm sure this case will have a . . . HOPPY . . . ending."

Mila groaned at my joke.

Stringbean frowned.

Even my dog, Rags, howled from the grass below.

Tough crowd.

Chapter Two

Frog City

"Let's visit the scene of the crime," I said to Stringbean and Mila.

Stringbean's eyes grew large. "The scene of the crime?"

"Yeah, your house," I explained.

"Why didn't you say so?" Stringbean asked.

Mila laughed. "That's typical Jigsaw. He loves saying stuff like that."

"You have to admit it," I said to Stringbean. "'Scene of the crime' sounds a lot cooler than 'Let's go to your house.'"

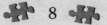

Stringbean nodded, thinking it over. "I don't think there's been a crime, Jigsaw. We're just talking about a missing frog."

"Just a missing frog," I repeated. "Sure, that's what they all say."

We rode our bikes to Stringbean's house. He lived over on Merkle Stream Drive. Right next to Lucy Hiller's house. I'd been over there more than a few times. Lucy and Stringbean had woods behind their houses. I once spent an afternoon back there trying to track down a grizzly bear — but that's another story.

There were a couple of trucks parked outside Stringbean's house, with a familiar white van in the driveway. There was lettering on the side of it:

TOM MOORE
Painting & Repair

I'd seen that van dozens of times around

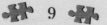 9

the neighborhood. That guy must have worked on every house in town.

The front door was open. Wide open. Men and women walked in and out of the house, carrying tools and equipment.

"Our house is a disaster area," Stringbean apologized. "We're turning the garage into a bedroom, finishing the basement, doing a whole new kitchen, and lots more."

The sound of hammering filled the house. "Noisy," Mila noted.

Stringbean nodded. "It's been like this for weeks," he complained. "It's driving my frogs crazy."

"It's not easy being green," I murmured.

Mila ignored me. "Did you say frogs?" she asked Stringbean. "Like, you've got more than one?"

"Oh, gosh, yes." Stringbean beamed. "Follow me."

As Mila and I followed him down a

hallway, Stringbean explained, "My parents are letting me keep them in our old TV room for now. The room is going to become my mom's home office," he said, opening a door. "But I still call it Frog City."

It was a small room, with low windows along two walls. I immediately noticed that

some of the
windows were
open.

In the middle of
the room sat a very large
plastic container filled
with — you guessed it — frogs.

The container also held about an inch
of water, and rocks and stuff. There was a
lid covering it, punctured with small holes
so the frogs could breathe, which seemed
like an awfully good idea. Frogs like air.

A man's deep voice startled me. "Showing off your froggies again?"

I spun around and saw a man hunched in the corner. He had a long white beard, wire-framed glasses, and a drill in his hand. He smiled, showing crooked teeth, and waved his hand.

"This is Tom Moore," Stringbean informed us. "Tom is like part of the

family. He's been Mr. Fix-it around here my whole life."

Tom Moore smiled. "That's right. They break it, I fix it. I'm just about done here," he told Stringbean. "I'll just finish packing up and be out of your way."

Stringbean reached into the container and picked up a frog. "Here, you wanna hold one, Jigsaw?"

I did not.

But that's just me. I'm not a real big fan of cold, wet, slimy things. Call me crazy.

Mila, on the other hand, was happy to grab a frog. She made a face. "Slippery." She laughed. "It's like trying to hold a bar of soap!"

"I always wondered," she said to Stringbean, "how can you tell the difference between a frog and a toad?"

Stringbean tucked in his shirt, pulled it out, then tucked it in all over again. It was a nervous habit, I guess. He was excited by

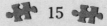

frogs. Go figure. "Of course, there are lots of different *kinds* of frogs," he told Mila. "The biggest frogs are from Africa. They are called Goliath frogs, and they grow to be as big as small dogs!"

Stringbean continued, "Frogs need to be wet. Toads are different. They are usually dry. They don't like to mess around in the water. A toad has rough skin, covered with little bumps like warts." He picked up another frog from the plastic container. "But there's one easy way to tell the difference between a frog and a toad," Stringbean said. "Watch."

Stringbean gently rubbed the frog's stomach, soothing it. Carefully, he set it down on the floor.

BOOOIIINNNGGG!

It jumped clear across the room!

"Toads walk," Stringbean said. "They don't jump."

"And frogs sure do!" Mila exclaimed, laughing.

Chapter Three
Kidnapped

While Stringbean's mother grilled cheese sandwiches in the kitchen, I grilled Stringbean with questions in the living room.

I checked the notes I had written in my journal. "The carpenter, Tom Moore, said to you: 'Showing off your froggies AGAIN?' Who else was over today?"

"People love seeing my frogs," Stringbean said. "There were a whole bunch of people."

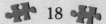

"Which people, exactly?" Mila asked.

I wrote down the names:

SUSPECTS
Bigs Maloney
Lucy Hiller
Eddie Becker
Sasha Mink

"We know most of the kids on the list

from school," Mila said. "But who is Sasha Mink?"

Stringbean held out his open palms. "Beats me. Some new kid in town. Lucy knows her from soccer or something."

I put a little star next to Sasha Mink's name.

"Is that when you noticed Adonis was missing?" I asked.

Stringbean shook his head. "Not really. The room was pretty crowded. There was a lot going on," he explained. "Frogs jumping all over the place. It's hard to keep track."

Mila noted, "So Adonis might have escaped then . . . or sometime after?"

Stringbean untucked his shirt, bunching up the ends in his fingers. "I don't know *when* Adonis disappeared. All I know for sure is that when I went back into Frog City about half an hour later, Adonis was definitely gone."

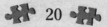

Mila nodded. "But it's *possible* that Adonis, er, *escaped*, at the time when everybody was visiting."

Stringbean bit his lip. "Yes, it's possible."

Mila looked at me. "Are you thinking what I'm thinking?" she asked.

"Are you thinking that you'd love a glass of grape juice?" I wondered.

"No," Mila said. "I'm thinking that maybe Adonis didn't escape after all."

"Oh," I mused. "I guess I was thinking about that, too, along with the grape juice."

"What do you mean, Adonis didn't escape?" Stringbean interrupted. "Of course he did. He's gone, isn't he?!"

"Calm down, Stringbean," I suggested. "It's very possible that Adonis was stolen."

"Stolen?!" Stringbean gulped. "But why?"

Mila pointed to the words at the bottom of the Frog-jumping Contest poster. She

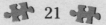 21

FROG JUMPING CONTEST
To be held Sunday, April 25, at 12:00
BRING YOUR OWN FROG!
Age 3-5 -- Can have some help in circle
-- Cannot be aided in any way
up -- Cannot be aided in
Trophies for 1st and 2nd
Ribbons for all
$20 Cash Prize for longest jump
* * * * *

read aloud: "Twenty-dollar Cash Prize for longest jump."

"The oldest motive in the world," I said. "Money."

Stringbean couldn't believe it. "But those are my friends," he said. "They wouldn't steal for it."

"Look, Stringbean," I explained patiently, "you said that Adonis could easily win that jumping contest. Right?"

"Right."

"But if Adonis isn't around to enter the contest . . ."

". . . then somebody else will win the money," Mila concluded. "We've been detectives for a long time, Stringbean," I said. "We've seen a lot of bad things. Some people, even people we think of as friends, will do *anything* for an extra dollar."

I stood up and rubbed my stomach. "First things first. There is one mystery

that I think you might be able to solve right now."

"There is?" Stringbean asked.

"Yeah," I replied. "What is taking your mother so long with those grilled cheese sandwiches? I'm starving."

Chapter Four
The Plan

"How do you like it?"

I held up the flier for Mila to see.

"Ummm, it's . . . er, good," Mila said. She didn't sound convincing.

I studied the flier.

"What's wrong with it?" I asked.

"That's a picture of a frog, right?" Mila asked.

"Right."

Mila squinched up her nose. "It looks like a wet sock with eyes."

"What do you want me to do?" I complained. "Glue on a picture of Kermit from *Sesame Street*?"

Mila smiled. "Maybe frogs aren't your strong point, Jigsaw. Let me try to draw the picture." Mila sat down and began to draw. "But if I ever need a really good picture of a sock, I'll know who to ask," she added.

I sighed. "This all seems like a waste of time."

"We have to try everything," Mila said. "You saw that open window in Frog City. It is possible that Adonis jumped to freedom."

"Yeah, like a prison escape," I said.

Mila got up to look for a picture of a frog that she could copy. She soon returned with a book, *The Tale of Jeremy Fisher* by Beatrix Potter.

"One of my all-time favorites," Mila purred. She picked up a green crayon.

Meanwhile, I paced the room. My dog, Rags, paced alongside me. I was thinking.

 27

He was drooling. I guess you could say we were a team.

"I'll call some friends, see if we can get help," Mila offered. "We'll search the neighborhood. Adonis couldn't have hopped very far. I'll go from house to house. Maybe somebody has seen him."

"Good idea," I said. "Talk to dog owners. They are always out walking their pets in the neighborhood. If there's a frog on the

loose, they might have seen it. I'll tell you what. Take Rags with you. Dogs are natural detectives. If he sniffs something, Rags will investigate. The problem is, he's more likely to find an old doughnut than a runaway frog."

Mila frowned. "Aren't you going to help?"

"There's not enough time," I replied. "We've got to split up. I have a lot of suspects to check out. Plus, I've got to find out more about this frog-jumping contest."

Mila finished her drawing of the frog. It looked pretty good. "There," she said. "Done."

Mila raced off to the library. She needed to make copies of the flier and tape them all over Stringbean's neighborhood.

I jumped on my bike.

I had suspects to meet and questions to ask them. Their names were Bigs Maloney, Lucy Hiller, Eddie Becker, and Sasha Mink.

I already knew Eddie, Bigs, and Lucy. They didn't seem like they'd ever steal from Stringbean.

But Sasha Mink?

That was a new one on me.

Chapter Five

Want to Bet?

I started with Eddie Becker. No reason, really. He lived the closest.

Eddie and I weren't real good friends, but we weren't enemies, either. Eddie loved two things: 1) baseball, and 2) money.

But not in that order.

Eddie was shooting hoops on the street outside his house. That's the great thing about basketball. It's a team sport that you can practice by yourself. Go figure.

I pulled up my bicycle at the foul line. "Hey, Eddie," I said.

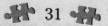

He nodded. Eyed the basket. And shot.

The ball bounced off the rim, up against the backboard, and slipped through the net.

"Lucky shot," I said.

"I'll make it again," Eddie said. "Bet ya."

Eddie loves to bet — and there isn't anything in the world he won't bet on. Two birds might be sitting on a telephone line. Eddie will bet which one will fly away first. He'll bet on a ball game or the color of the next car that drives down the street. The weirder the bet, the happier he is. He is just one of those guys who needs to keep things interesting. Like regular life isn't quite enough for him. Nah, there has to be something riding on it.

I gave Eddie a quarter after he made the shot.

"Double or nothing?" Eddie offered.

"Not today, Eddie." I squinted into the sun. "I'm working on a case. Tell you the truth, I have a couple of questions for you."

Eddie twirled the basketball on his finger. "Sure, Jigsaw. Ask away."

Eddie admitted that he had been

in Stringbean's house that morning.

"Sure, I saw Adonis," Eddie said. "That's why I was there. I had heard about that frog. I wanted to see if the stories were true."

"Oh?"

"Yeah," Eddie said. "There's the frog-jumping contest tomorrow. I was thinking of placing a bet."

I didn't say anything about that. But it got my wheels spinning. "Are you entering the contest?" I asked.

Eddie bounced the ball between his legs. Real smooth. "No, that's not my thing," he said. "Too much work. Besides, I can get more out of it by betting on the right frog. Why are you asking?"

I told him that Adonis was missing.

Eddie's mouth opened. I could tell that it was the first time he was hearing about it. "Really? Wow, that changes things."

"Thinking of changing your bet?" I asked.

Eddie smiled. "That's my business, Jigsaw. But, well, yeah. That Adonis — man, that frog can jump. But now I might have to bet on another frog."

"Like who?" I asked.

Eddie's eyes twinkled. He didn't bite.

"I'm not going to tell anybody," I said to him. "I'm just curious. Now that Adonis is out of the way, whose frog do you think has the best chance?"

"Well, the best frog trainer in town is Slim Palmer. He's a legend. The guy knows more about frogs than anybody on the planet. But Slim is about fourteen. For ages six to nine, I like a frog named Brooklyn."

"Whose frog is that?" I wondered.

"New girl," Eddie said. "Sasha Something."

"Mink," I said. "Sasha Mink."

Eddie winked. "That's the one," he said. "Kind of cute, too, if you like freckles. She moved into that big house on the corner of Penny Lane and Abbey Road."

I thanked Eddie. Five seconds later, I was on my way.

Chapter Six

Sasha Mink

I recognized Lucy Hiller from down the block. Who else would wear red go-go boots, pink stockings, a white skirt, and a lavender glitter jacket?

As I pedaled closer to Lucy's house, I took a good look at the new girl. Her blond hair was tied back with something that my sister calls a scrunchie. She looked pretty regular to me. But that's okay. I'm a regular kind of guy.

I slid off my bicycle and put down the kickstand.

"Hi, Jigsaw," Lucy greeted me. "This is my friend Sasha."

Sasha smiled warmly. She reached out her hand. "It's nice to meet you . . . Jigsaw." She paused. "I think you're the first Jigsaw I've ever met."

I shrugged. "Yeah, well, I guess you don't get around much."

"Ignore him, Sasha," Lucy said. "Jigsaw can be a little weird sometimes. Let's do that hand-clap rhyme you taught me yesterday."

"Actually, I'm here on business," I said. "I have a couple of questions I need to ask you. But I'll wait. Do your hand-clap thing first."

So they did. And I'll tell you, it was something else. Mila would have loved it. They clapped, and tapped elbows, and did all sorts of moves with their hands. The words went like this:

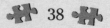 38

*"This is a game
of concentration.
No repeats
or hesitation.
I'll go first,
and you'll go next.
The category is . . .
the Seven Dwarfs!"*

Then they took turns naming one dwarf at a time. Which isn't simple. Sure, Sleepy and Sneezy are easy. But everybody forgets Doc and Bashful. Try it sometime, you'll see.

Anyway, every time Lucy and Sasha did the rhyme, they changed the category. It could be names of cars, baseball teams, kids in school, whatever.

Then it was time to get down to business.

"I heard you guys were at Stringbean's

house this morning," I began. "It seems like somebody may have hopped off with his best frog."

"Adonis?" Sasha asked.

"That's the one," I said.

"What happened to him?" Lucy wondered.

"That's what I'm trying to find out," I replied. "*Poof!* He just mysteriously vanished. Maybe he ran away. Maybe a cat ate him. I don't know."

"Yuck, Jigsaw!" Lucy exclaimed. "Don't talk like that."

"Okay, okay," I said. "It was just that —"

"We better get over there and help Stringbean look for him," Sasha interrupted. "That poor frog, lost and alone."

Lucy agreed. Like she thought it was the greatest idea on earth.

"That would be nice of you guys," I said. "Mila is searching the neighborhood now.

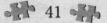

But let me ask you: Are you *sure* you didn't see anything strange?"

Sasha laughed. "That carpenter was pretty strange," she said. "But he was funny, too. I don't know, Jigsaw. There were a lot of workers in and out of that house. Frogs were jumping around like crazy. I guess Adonis got lost in the confusion."

"I guess so," I replied.

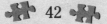

Before they left, Sasha turned and asked me, "Are you going to enter the contest, Jigsaw?"

"I, uh — no, no, I don't think so. I mean" — I turned my pockets inside out — "it's not like I own a frog or anything."

"You should," Sasha said. "It's a lot of fun."

And that gave me an idea.

"Maybe I will," I said. "You never know."

Chapter Seven

To Catch a Frog

Slim Palmer was nice enough to meet me at a place called Twin Lakes. That's right, it's two lakes that look the same. "Twin" lakes.

Slim was one of those impossibly thin guys, elbows and long legs sticking out all over the place. Like a scarecrow made of sticks and stuffed with spaghetti.

He wore muddy jeans and a muddy T-shirt. And no shoes.

I told Slim about the case. How there was a missing frog — how maybe it escaped, or

 44

maybe it was stolen — and that I needed to find it. But just as important, I needed to enter tomorrow's frog-jumping contest. I had to keep an eye on things. To do that, I needed a frog. Slim agreed to help me.

Slim wore a straw hat over his dirty blond hair. Yes, the hat was muddy, too. *Everything* about Slim Palmer was muddy. "Look at me, Jigsaw," he said, "right here. Look me in the eyes."

Slim waited until I stared directly into his eyes.

"You're going about this case all wrong," Slim told me. "First thing you got to do is you got to start *thinking* like a frog."

"Thinking like a frog?" I repeated.

"Exactamundo," Slim said with a sharp nod.

"Ribbit," I croaked.

"I'm not joking," Slim protested. "Frogs are serious creatures. They don't joke around."

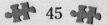 45

A mosquito hovered nearby. I tried to zap it with my sticky tongue. No luck. I wondered out loud, "How am I supposed to think like a frog?"

"First, you've got to educate yourself about frogs," Slim said. "That's why we're here. You and me are going frog hunting."

"It sounds . . . wet," I noted.

A broad grin filled Slim's face. "Wet . . . and *buggy*," he said. "Just the way frogs like it."

The last light of day was fading. Dusk gathered around the edges of the lake. "Getting dark," Slim noted. "That's good. Usually, I like to catch frogs in the darkest time of night. I use a flashlight and it works just fine. The bright light sort of puts those frogs in what you call a hypnotic trance. I figure it's because a flashlight is about the most amazing thing a frog has seen in its entire life. Like if you looked up and saw a spaceship land in your rose garden. I guess

you'd stand there frozen solid, too. Isn't that right, Jigsaw? You see a spaceship come out of the sky, what would you do?"

I told Slim that I probably would not do a whole lot.

"That's right," Slim said. "Just like a frog. *Shhhh!*"

Slim held up a hand. "Hear that?" he whispered. He took a deep smell, letting the air fill his chest. "Spring nights. Those frogs are calling out to each other."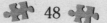

We listened for a long while. We heard croaks and froggy groans. But also screeches and the odd plunk of water.

Slim took a burlap bag and slowly,

silently soaked it in the lake. "You want it to be nice and wet," Slim whispered.

Slim handed me the burlap bag. Yeesh. He turned on his flashlight and walked out into the water. Pants and everything. All soaking wet. Then Slim Palmer headed into the tall grasses on the edges of the water.

He stopped and looked at me.

"You coming?" he asked.

"Coming?" I croaked. "In there?"

Slim laughed.

"You're not thinking like a frog," Slim chided. "'Cause if you were a real good detective, and if you were thinking like a frog, well, hey, you'd hop right in."

I sighed.

I kicked off my sneakers and socks.

I rolled up my pants.

And stepped into the gross lake.

Mom was not going to be happy about this.

Chapter Eight

The Frog Whisperer

Slim shone the flashlight along the bank. He stopped when the light landed on a frog, like a spotlight on a stage. Slim crept closer toward the frog.

As he walked, Slim whispered to the frog, making strange noises with his throat. I don't know what he said to that frog. But for some reason, it sat there and stared. Slim slowly reached out. He grabbed the frog, gently and firmly, in his hand. The frog didn't struggle or squirm. It was weird. Like the frog trusted Slim.

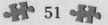

I held open the burlap bag, and Slim placed the frog into it. "He's a good-looking bullfrog, that's what he is," Slim whispered. "Looks like a real fine jumper, too."

Slim and I walked home together, at least most of the way. All the while, we talked about frogs. Or Slim talked. I listened. "So, detective," Slim finally said. "How come frogs are so good at baseball?"

I thought about it for a minute. "Because they like to catch flies," I guessed.

Slim laughed. "Maybe you're pretty smart after all. Even if you don't know much about frogs."

We paused under a streetlight. "I go this way," Slim said, pointing down the road. "I'll be seeing you at the frog-jumping contest tomorrow."

"I guess so," I managed to say.

"Oh, don't you worry," Slim said. "You'll be fine. Just remember what I said. You

have to be *kind* to that frog. Treat him nice, like he's your little brother or something. A happy frog is a good jumping frog. You have to love him. A frog gets scared or nervous, he'll jump sideways, backways, anyways. You'll never win nothing with a jittery frog."

I thanked Slim. I didn't have the heart to tell him that I didn't really care about winning the contest. I was a detective, working on a case. I figured the best way I could keep an eye on things was right there in the middle of the frog-jumping contest. If somebody was willing to steal a frog to win twenty dollars, who knows what else they might be willing to do?

Just the same, while I walked home I held that wet burlap bag close to my face. And I talked to that frog, nice and easy, all the way home.

I hoped he was happy.

That night, I took a long bath. I talked to Mila on the portable phone. They never found Adonis. "We looked everywhere," Mila said. "Lucy, Sasha, Stringbean, everybody tried so hard."

Mila sounded tired.

"How's Stringbean feeling?" I asked.

"He's still got hope," Mila said. "He says that if anybody can find Adonis, it's Jigsaw Jones."

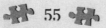

Hearing that should have made me feel good inside.

But instead, I just slipped deeper into the water.

And stared at the ceiling.

For a long, long time.

Chapter Nine

Never Give Up

Have you ever heard how somebody "woke up on the wrong side of the bed"?

It happened to me.

Now my nose hurts.

My dog, Rags, was snuggled on my bed, snoring. That's right, I've got a dog that snores. Rags took up most of the bed. He's more hog than dog. I was squished like a ham sandwich in a crowded backpack.

Here, I'll draw a picture. This is what I looked like with my face smashed up against the wall:

No, it wasn't pretty.

That's what I call waking up on the wrong side of the bed.

I even had dog fur in my mouth. *Ptew!* That's when I noticed the slime on the back of my neck. If there's one thing I don't like, it's slime. For Rags, slime is a special talent. Some dogs fetch slippers. Others bay at the moon. My dog drools. He would have made a good frog. Wet and gross.

Sigh.

Then I remembered it was Sunday. The day of the frog-jumping contest. I checked the clock. It read 7:14. My heart sank. I only had a few more hours before noon.

A few more hours before I had to tell Stringbean Noonan that I couldn't find his frog. Before I had to say, "Sorry, pal. Jigsaw Jones just struck out."

I climbed out of bed, fumbled over Rags

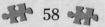

(he decided to sleep late), and checked out how my frog was doing. I had put him in my closet last night with a pan full of water.

Slim said it was important to keep the frog wet. "You don't want a dry frog," he said. "They don't jump so good when they're dead."

That Slim. He got right to the point.

During breakfast, I tried to think of a plan. I figured I might as well head over to Stringbean's for one last look around.

That's when Mila called.

"Jigsaw, are you ready to go?" she asked.

I muttered a reply.

"What's wrong with you?" she asked.

"I don't know," I said. "Just sleepy, I guess. This case has gotten me down."

"Snap out of it, Jigsaw," Mila demanded. Her voice was suddenly firm and strong. "You remember the first rule in detective work, don't you? *Never give up. Don't ever give up.*"

"You're right," I said.

"That's right, I'm right," Mila shot back. "Hurry up and get dressed. I'm coming over in ten minutes. We've got a mystery to solve." Five minutes later, the phone rang again.

It was Sasha Mink.

"I think I remember something," she told me.

 61

Chapter Ten

A Piece Falls into Place

When you've been a detective for as long as I have, it can mess up your head. You begin to think that *everybody* is a suspect. That everybody is capable of doing something really rotten.

It can get to you after a while. You kind of sour on people.

This whole case was like that. I could only think the worst about people. But maybe it wasn't that way at all. Maybe nobody had done anything wrong.

So far on this case, I had met two new

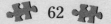 62

people: Sasha Mink and Slim Palmer. And you know what? They were both really nice. Not bad guys. But good guys.

The question is, *How does this help me solve the case?*

Sasha, Mila, and I met at Stringbean's house. It was 9:47, Sunday morning. The frog-jumping contest was only two hours away.

"Sasha may have remembered an important clue," I told Stringbean.

He looked from me to Sasha.

"I remember that you closed the windows before taking the lid off the frog container," Sasha said.

"Are you sure?" Stringbean asked.

Sasha nodded. "Absolutely. There's no way that a frog jumped out the window."

Stringbean pulled on the edges of his shirt. "But then how did Adonis escape? Somebody must have stolen him."

"Maybe not," I said to Stringbean. "Let's

say, just this once, that there's no bad guy."

I continued, "Maybe Adonis got taken . . . by accident."

Stringbean made a face. "Who would *accidentally* take a frog? That's crazy."

"Maybe," I said. "But it's all we've got."

Mila suddenly snapped her fingers. "That carpenter guy . . ."

"Tom Moore," I said. "The missing piece to our puzzle."

Mila grabbed my detective journal. She quickly read through my notes. "Tom Moore was packing things up," Mila said. "He was going in and out of the room . . . loading up his van!"

"Loading up his van?" Stringbean wondered. "Do you think Adonis jumped into one of his toolboxes?"

I could see the excitement on Stringbean's face.

"We've got to call Tom Moore," I said. "He might have Adonis . . . and not even know it!"

Chapter Eleven

Adonis

Tom Moore drove over as soon as we called him. He opened the back doors of his van. He jumped out of the van and quickly opened the back doors.

Stringbean held up a hand to his ear. He listened.

"Adonis?" he called out.

Then louder: "ADONIS?"

A faint sound, the softest croak, came in reply.

Stringbean pointed excitedly. "In there! In there!"

Tom Moore, scratching his white beard, climbed into the van. He slid a large toolbox toward the edge.

We opened it up.

And there was Adonis.

"You did it, Jigsaw!" Sasha exclaimed. She and Mila high-fived.

But Stringbean's smile soon turned to a look of worry. "He's sick," Stringbean whispered.

"Adonis is dry," I noted, remembering

the words of Slim Palmer. "Frogs need to be moist."

Stringbean carried Adonis into his house. "I'm going to call the vet," he said. "I think he'll be okay."

"What about the contest?" Sasha asked.

Stringbean paused. He held Adonis so delicately in his hands. "Not today," Stringbean said. "The contest isn't important. I'm just going to take care of Adonis today."

And then, right before he closed the door, Stringbean called out, "Thanks, Jigsaw."

I smiled. Being a detective is hard work. But nothing tops the feeling of solving a case.

Mila grabbed my elbow. "Let's jet," she said. "There's still time to get to the frog-jumping contest!"

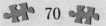

Chapter Twelve

The Contest

I named my frog Flubber. You know, that bouncy stuff from the Disney movie.

I should have named him something different. Something like Sleepy or Dopey. You get the idea.

We didn't exactly win first prize.

For the contest, there's a big "jumping area," which is just a brightly colored sheet. There are circles of different colors on the sheet, like a target.

You are supposed to place your frog in the middle of the smallest circle. The frog

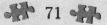

is allowed to take three jumps away from the center. Then the judges measure the distance it traveled. If the frog jumps three times in a straight line, it can go pretty far!

Easy, right?

Except my frog didn't jump. It sat.

"He's thinking," I explained to the judges.

After a while, we gave up.

Slim Palmer came up to me. "Sorry, Jigsaw," he said with a big smile. "I guess I found you the laziest frog in town."

I didn't mind.

Slim had a trophy tucked under his arm. He was the day's big winner.

"Hey, you and your friends want to come to the lakes with me?" Slim asked. He looked at Bigs and Mila, Lucy and Sasha. "I'm in charge of putting all these frogs back into Twin Lakes. After all, that's where a frog ought to live."

"Sounds muddy," Mila said.

"Sounds wet," I said.

"Sounds GREAT!" everybody roared.

About the Author

James Preller often draws upon his own life as a basis for his Jigsaw Jones books. Like Jigsaw, James Preller has a slobbering, sock-eating dog. Like Jigsaw, James was the youngest in a large family. His older brothers called him Worm and worse — yeesh! And so do Jigsaw's!

James and Jigsaw both love jigsaw puzzles, baseball, grape juice, and mysteries! But even though Jigsaw and James have so much in common, they are not the same person.

Unlike Jigsaw, James Preller is the author of more than 80 books for children, including *The Big Book of Picture-Book Authors & Illustrators*; *Wake Me in Spring*; *Hiccups for Elephant*, and *Cardinal & Sunflower*. He lives in Delmar, New York, with his wife, Lisa, three kids —Nicholas, Gavin, and Maggie — his cat, Blue, and his dog, Seamus.

Take your imagination on a wild ride.

THE SECRETS ~OF~ DROON

Under the stairs, a magical world awaits you.

Ghostville Elementary™

Welcome to Sleepy Hollow Elementary. Everyone says the basement is haunted, but no one's ever gone downstairs to prove it. Until now. This year, Jeff and Cassidy's classroom is moving to the basement. And you thought your school was scary!

BOO!

BLACK LAGOON ADVENTURES

Visit a school where class trips are nightmares, talent shows are frightful, and school elections have students running for their lives. With teachers like Coach Kong, classes at the Black Lagoon are so funny…it's scary.

Available wherever you buy books.

www.scholastic.com

LITTLE APPLE

SCHOLASTIC